Stolen Treasure

ANNE SCHRAFF

SADDLEBACK
EDUCATIONAL PUBLISHING

red rhino
books™

With more titles on the way ...

SADDLEBACK
EDUCATIONAL PUBLISHING
www.sdlback.com

ISBN-13: 978-1-62250-902-7
ISBN-10: 1-62250-902-1
eBook: 978-1-63078-034-0

Printed in Guangzhou, China
NOR/0714/CA21401177

18 17 16 15 14   1 2 3 4 5

Isa

Age: 10

First Crush: Mikey Alvarez from third grade

Dream School: Harvard

Favorite Flowers: pink peonies and
green spider mums

Best Quality: compassion

RAFe

Age: 18

Favorite Movie: *Dogtown and Z-Boys*

Future Plans: would like to be an electrician

Favorite Skating Music: punk rock

Best Quality: cares about his mother's feelings

1

IT'S GONE

Ten-year-old Isa Rodriguez heard her mom scream. The sound came from the living room. Isa rushed to her mother. "Mom! Mom! What's the matter?" Isa cried.

Mom was standing in the middle of the room. She was pale. "It's gone!" she cried. "It's gone!"

It's Gone!

↖ our family's frame for over 150 years!

Isa looked at the wall. Her mother was pointing there. "Grandma's picture!" Isa gasped. It had always hung there. Over the mantel. It wasn't there.

Grandpa hired an artist. The artist painted a picture of Grandma. Grandpa wanted to give Grandma a great birthday present. Something beautiful. He saved money for a long time. It was the most beautiful picture Isa had ever seen.

I'm named after my grandmother

Ten years. That's how long it hung on the wall. It was the family's greatest treasure.

"What happened?" Isa asked. "It was there last night. My friends came over. They looked at it."

"I don't know," Mom sobbed.

Grandma had kept the painting at her house. Until ten years ago. Then she gave it to her youngest daughter. That was Isa's mother.

Maria

Tati

Isa's mom was Maria. Maria's older sister was Tati. Tati wanted to keep the picture

3

in her house. She was sad when Grandma gave it to Maria. Tati was mad at Maria too. Grandma thought Maria was the best. She gave Maria the picture.

"Who could have taken it?" Isa cried. The picture was beautiful. But it was not worth a lot of money.

Just then, Dad came in the room. "What's the yelling about?" he asked.

"Oh, Ric," Mom said. "Somebody stole Mom's picture!"

"Stole it?" Dad said. "That's crazy. Who would do that? Nobody broke in here last night. The door is still locked."

Double locked!

"But it's gone," Mom said. She was crying. "That picture. It was the most prized thing in our family. It was special. Dad gave mom the picture. He died right after that. He was a Marine. He got sent to war. He died for our country. It was his last gift."

the last gift

love notes

Marine seal

Isa knew the sad story. She began to cry too. How could it be gone?

Dad looked at the wall. There was just a nail. The picture was not secure. But nobody thought it had to be. Who would steal it?

Isa's nine-year-old brother came into the living room. "What's up, you guys?" Eddie rubbed sleep from his eyes. The noise had woken him up.

Isa looked at her little brother. They got along okay. Most of the time. But he could be a pest too.

Eddie, sometimes a pest

"Somebody stole Grandma's picture last night," Isa said.

"Stole it?" Eddie said. "Why? It's old. Any windows broken?" Then he made a funny face. He looked at Isa. "You had those girls over. They were here last night. Maybe one of them took it. Kit Shaw. Everybody at school says she's a thief."

Isa gasped. "Eddie! How can you say that? Kit would never do that."

No one else came over last night. It was just Isa's friends. They made bracelets. Kit Shaw, Gina Luna, and Sandy Alvarez were her BFFs.

BFFs

Kit was Isa's favorite. Isa knew the gossip about Kit. She didn't believe it. Some girl who didn't like Kit started it. Isa hated lies. Plus, she knew Kit's heart. It was honest.

Gina Luna was jealous of Isa. They

always competed. Isa usually won. Gina didn't like that. But they were still friends. There was a lot to like about Gina. Isa tried to overlook the jealousy.

Sandy Alvarez was a nice girl. Her family was poor. She dressed badly. Hm. But that didn't mean anything. Did it?

Isa glanced at Mom. Her eyes were big. Her mom was thinking something. She was thinking one of Isa's friends could have done it. No way!

2
WAS IT KIT?

"Honey," Mom said slowly. "I know your friends are good girls. But they *were* here last night. What I'm thinking is—"

"Mom," Isa cried. "How can you even think that? No way! My friends do not steal. They know we love that picture. They would *never* steal it!" Tears ran down Isa's face.

"Well," Dad said in a serious voice. "Somebody took it. Call the girls. Ask them if they saw anything. Heard anything. It can't hurt."

"Oh, Ric," Mom groaned. "Mom is coming to dinner. On Sunday. I can't take it. She will be so sad. She'll see it's gone. And she'll cry."

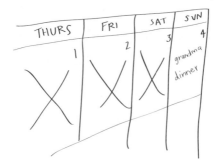

"I guess we better call the cops," Eddie said. He thought it would be pretty exciting. The police coming in. Looking around. Asking questions.

"The police!" Mom cried. "Nobody broke

into the house. The doors were locked. I checked before going to bed. I always check."

Dad turned to Isa. "Isa, why not just call your friends? Tell them what happened. Kids sometimes do dumb things. Maybe it's a trick."

Isa was shocked. Dad thought her friends did something. Knew something. Stole the picture. Really? How could that be? A cold fear came over her. What if it was true?

"Everybody at school says Kit steals," Eddie said.

"That's a lie!" Isa yelled.

Eddie backed off. "Maybe it was a joke. Or something. Like Dad says."

Isa knew what her parents were thinking. Maybe Kit *was* a thief. Maybe Gina was sick of Isa winning. Getting praise. Maybe Gina decided to hurt Isa. Maybe Sandy was tired of being poor. So tired that she decided to steal. The picture looked expensive.

Isa went to her room. She called Kit first. "Hi, Kit. About last night. Something bad happened at our house. To my grandma's picture. Somebody took it. We feel awful. I was just wondering. Maybe you heard or saw something."

There was a long silence. When Kit finally spoke, she sounded angry. "Wow. Really, Isa? Any time something goes missing? Everybody looks at me. But, silly me. I thought we were close. I didn't think you believed the talk. I thought we were best friends, Isa. I guess I was wrong."

Kit sounded like she was crying. Isa's heart sank.

3
WAS IT SANDY?

"Kit," Isa cried. "I'm not saying you did anything. I know you didn't. I trust you. I always have. I always will. But Mom and Dad wanted me to call. I'm calling all of you. Gina and Sandy too. Maybe you heard something. Did you notice anything? Maybe when we were making bracelets?"

"I'm sorry for freaking on you, Isa," Kit said in a softer voice. "It's just … I'm so sick of always being picked on. I'm honest. I never stole anything. Ever."

"I know," Isa said. "But maybe you noticed something."

Sandy's
Family Dinner

"Well, uh, I hate to say this. The talk about me has hurt. A lot. I hate to be a gossip too. But you know what? Sandy's family is poor. Really poor. She told me they have cereal for dinner. Sometimes. Well, last night? Sandy went out on the back patio. A couple times. She said she was looking at the full moon. She said it was really pretty. But I sorta wondered. I mean, that picture looks expensive. If you're really poor? If you don't know? Maybe you think it's worth something," Kit said.

Full Moon Last Night

Isa felt bad about what Kit said. But maybe she was right. Poor Sandy. It was hard to be so poor. "Well, Kit, I'm calling the others now. Thanks."

Gina lived down the street from Isa. The girls rode the school bus together. Gina was not a close friend. That was because Gina was jealous of Isa.

Isa was very pretty. She had short dark hair. She always looked nice. Gina was plainer. She never got her hair right. Her clothes never looked as good. Gina was jealous of other things too. Isa made better grades in school. Isa was always picked first for things. Like the lead in the school play, *The Wizard of Oz*.

It was sort of that way with Isa's mom and aunt. Aunt Tati was always jealous of Mom. Mom was prettier. Smarter. Mom lived in a big house. Aunt Tati's family lived in a small house.

our house

Aunt Tati's house

Mom and Tati competed. All the time. Grandma made Aunt Tati mad. How could she give the picture to Maria? Tati was the oldest. She was upset about the picture.

Isa felt bad about how her aunt felt. She felt bad about how Gina felt too. She texted Gina. Gina hadn't seen anything. Like Kit, she tattled on Sandy.

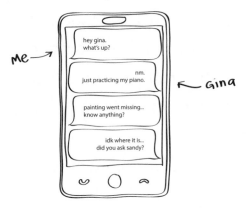

Isa sighed. She called Sandy. No answer. The phone just rang. And rang. And rang. Sandy did not have a cell phone. Isa could not text her. It would have to wait. Tomorrow she would talk to Sandy. At school.

Dad reported the stolen picture to the police. A police officer came. He looked at the wall where the picture had been. He looked for clues. He checked the backyard for footprints. Then he wrote a report and left.

Mom sat in the living room. She stared at the empty spot on the wall. Tears dripped from her eyes. Isa felt so sorry for her.

"How will I tell my mom her picture is gone? She's coming over for Sunday dinner," Mom groaned.

Isa sat beside her mom on the couch. She put her arm around her. "Maybe something good will happen. Let's hope and pray," Isa said.

4
THE GARDENER

The next day was school. Isa saw Sandy before class. As usual, Sandy was wearing old clothes. Her big sister's. She looked shabby. Isa felt sorry for her.

sandy wears baggy hand-me-downs

Isa told Sandy about the stolen picture.

Sandy gave Isa a hug. "I'm so sorry, Isa. I know how much you love your grandma. I know how much she loves that picture. I always thought it was so pretty."

"Grandma is coming Sunday for dinner. She will see it's gone. She'll be heartbroken," Isa said. "Remember I told you my grandpa was a Marine? He died in an attack in Lebanon. The picture was his last gift to her."

Grandma's broken heart →

"I wish I had something to tell you," Sandy said. "I didn't see anything that night. We were having fun making bracelets. But …"

"But what, Sandy?" Isa asked.

"Well, it's probably nothing. I went out on the patio. Your gardener was clipping the bushes," Sandy said.

"We don't have a gardener," Isa said.

"No?" Sandy's eyes widened.

But we don't have a gardener!

"Well, someone was out there. I saw him. The moon was so bright. It was around eight. I thought it was weird at first. But then I figured the moonlight helped. You know? To see what he was doing."

"What did this guy look like?" Isa asked.

23

Her heart was pounding.

"Just a young guy. Maybe eighteen. Or even younger. Long hair. There was a skateboard against the shed," Sandy said. "It was probably nothing."

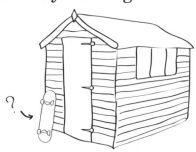

"Thanks, Sandy," Isa said. "It's something to look into."

It was after school. Isa walked toward her house. She saw Aunt Tati's car in the driveway. She could hear yelling. Heated words were coming from inside. Like dark smoke. Isa went in. Walked toward the voices.

"I can't believe you lost our treasure! The picture was important to me. To our family. Mom trusted you with Dad's last gift!" Aunt Tati screamed.

"Tati," Mom cried. "I didn't lose it. It was stolen!"

"How could that happen?" Aunt Tati demanded. "How?" She frowned. "You don't lock your doors at night? You are careless. Look! The sliding doors are wide open. Anyone can come in from the back. This is not safe! You're too lazy to lock the doors."

Mom wiped away her tears. "A terrible

thing has happened," she said. "Do we have to make it worse by fighting?"

Mama's Pet

Pretty Little Maria

Always Perfect

Does NO wrong

"Well, you better tell Mom. *You* break her heart!" Aunt Tati snapped. "I guess it's her own fault. Trusting you with the picture. You always were her little pet. Maria could do no wrong. Pretty little Maria was perfect. Well, see what Maria has done now. She has let Dad's last gift to Mom be stolen!"

Aunt Tati seemed almost happy about what had happened.

5

AUNT TATI'S MAD

Aunt Tati stomped out of the house. Slammed the front door. She got into her old car. She drove fast down the driveway. Her tires squealed.

SCREECH

Isa sat next to her mom. Mom was staring at the empty space. Again. She was crying. Isa sat beside her. "I heard Aunt Tati being mean. You could hear her down the street! I'm sorry, Mom. I'm sorry she yelled."

"No," Mom said. "My sister is right. It's my fault the picture is gone. It shouldn't have been so easy. I should have treated it like a treasure. It *is* a treasure. Now it's gone. Sometimes I do leave the sliding doors open. I'm careless. Tati is right. I wouldn't hurt Mom for the world. Now look what I've done."

Not like this—
Our treasure is better!

"Mom, guess what? Today, Sandy told me something weird. About the other night. The night the picture vanished. There was a guy in our backyard. He was clipping the bushes. Sandy thought he was our gardener," Isa said.

Mom turned. Her eyes were wide. "We've never had a gardener. Your dad loves to do that stuff himself. Did Sandy recognize him?"

"No. She said he was young. He had long hair. He had a skateboard. It was leaning on the shed," Isa said. "It was kinda dark. She didn't see him real good. There was moonlight. But he was working in the shadows."

Isa and her dad liked to walk. After dinner they took their usual path. They liked the sidewalks in their neighborhood. But it wasn't a normal walk. There was a dark cloud hanging over them.

"Your mom is taking this hard, Isa," Dad said.

"Yeah. And Aunt Tati was mean today," Isa said. "It's like she hates Mom."

"That's an old, sad story," Dad said. "Jealousy. The green-eyed monster. Your grandma loves both her girls. Exactly the same.

Jealousy. The Green-eyed Monster.

"But your mom was sweeter. Everybody made a fuss over her. Poor Tati got more and more jealous. It ate at her."

"Like my friend Gina," Isa said. "I like Gina so much. We have fun together. I want to be better friends with her. But Gina is

31

jealous. I get better scores. Gina gets mad. She said I'm the teacher's pet. Sometimes she won't talk to me for days. And the school play? I got to be Dorothy in *The Wizard of Oz*. Gina really wanted it. She stopped talking to me for a week!"

They walked around the corner. And they headed home.

"It's so terrible. That picture was Grandpa's last gift," Isa said.

"Yeah," Dad said. "He was home on leave. Then he was sent to Lebanon. There was a war there. He never came home."

Grandpa had signed the painting. His note was on the back. Isa remembered reading it.

"To the most beautiful girl in the world. For Isabel Avila. My sweetheart, *mi esposa*. Forever my love. Eduardo Avila."

6
ART CONTEST

There was exciting news. Mr. Murray said there was an art contest. The school was having an open house. The best artist in each grade would paint a school poster. Isa began to raise her hand. She was a good artist. Then she stopped.

Gina was a good artist too. It looked like

she wanted to win. She wanted to make the open house poster. She was waving her hand in the air. She seemed really excited. Then she glanced over at Isa. She thought Isa would be competing too. Mr. Murray would pick the best entry.

Gina was afraid Isa would beat her. Again. Just like she did in every test. Just like she did in the tryouts for the play. Just like she did in everything. Gina frowned. Isa saw.

Mr. Murray looked at Isa. He knew she was a good artist. "Are you going to try out for the poster, Isa?" he asked. Mr. Murray knew both girls had talent. He thought one would win.

"No, Mr. Murray," Isa said. "I'm kinda tired of art. I'm learning to play guitar."

I want to jam!

"Oh," Mr. Murray said. "Well then, I'm anxious to see your entry, Gina."

Gina almost jumped up and down with excitement. She had so many ideas. She thought her poster would be the best. Better than any other entry. The best in the school. "I'll do a great job, Mr. Murray," Gina cried. "I'll get started tonight. Right after school!"

Isa had not seen Gina so happy in a long time. Isa wanted to make a poster. It would have been fun. And maybe she would have won. But having Gina for a friend was more important. More important than winning.

Gina walked from class with Isa. They headed for the bus.

"What kind of poster are you going to make?" Isa asked.

"Oh, I've got the coolest idea. You know how everybody loves pandas? Well, I'm going to dress them up like moms and dads.

And they're coming to the school's open house!"

"That sounds cool," Isa said.

"Why didn't you enter? I was surprised," Gina said. "You're such a good artist."

"Oh. I like music better now," Isa lied.

Gina's smile faded. "Anything new about your grandma's picture? I feel so bad for you guys."

"No. I'm praying hard. Mom is super sad. She blames herself. Mom's older sister blames her too. Aunt Tati wanted to keep the painting in her house. She was mad Mom got to have it," Isa said.

"I sure hope you guys get it back," Gina

said. She gave Isa a hug. She hadn't done that in a long time.

On the bus, Isa and Gina sat together as usual. Gina was like her old self, talking away. She had a chance to win. That one fact made her happy.

Isa wondered something. Did Grandma ever see how hurt Aunt Tati was? How jealous she was. Grandma was a loving person. She would have done something if she had known.

7
CHECKERS

"See you tomorrow," Gina said. "Wait! Okay if I come over tonight? Show you how my poster is coming along?"

"Sure," Isa said. They got off the bus. Isa went one way. Gina another.

Last off the bus!

Isa ran up to her door. Dad was already

home from work. "Your mom's gone shopping," he said. "She was sad. Moping around the house. I told her to go to the mall. That always cheers her up. Nothing like full shopping bags to get your mind off stuff." Dad smiled at Isa. "How was school?"

↰ Retail Therapy

"It was good, Dad," Isa said. "Remember last night? I told you how Gina is always jealous of me. Well, Mr. Murray wanted us to do posters for open house. For a contest."

"That sounds like something you'd love," Dad said.

"Yeah, well. This time I decided not to enter. Gina wanted to do the poster. I could see it on her face. I didn't want to take a chance. You know? That I'd win. I don't want her always feeling bad 'cause I win," Isa said.

"I'm proud of you for doing that. Caring for somebody else's feelings. Now that's lots more important than winning a contest," Dad said.

"Yeah," Isa said.

Dad grinned. "Remember when you were younger? We'd play checkers."

"That was fun," Isa said. "I won a lot too."

Dad was still grinning. "I let you win sometimes. I didn't want you to always be the loser."

"Yeah, I guess I knew. I kinda figured it out," Isa said. "But I still liked to win. Even though you were losing on purpose."

Mom came home. She wasn't carrying shopping bags. Usually she had a lot of bags. Stuff for Dad. Stuff for Eddie. Stuff for Isa. And even stuff for herself. Isa felt sad. Mom was still upset about the picture. She couldn't even enjoy shopping. She didn't have the heart to buy anything.

Eddie came in from skateboarding. "I saw Rafe," he said. "I haven't seen him in a long time. He and some other big dudes were doing tricks. At the skate park."

Rafe was Aunt Tati's only child. The cousins had never been close. The bad feelings between Aunt Tati and Mom spilled over. Rafe always seemed angry.

"Rafe's mom told him about Grandma's picture being missing," Eddie said. "His mom said we were careless. That's why it happened." Eddie frowned. "Rafe seemed glad about what went down. He said we have good luck all the time. He said it was time we had some bad luck."

"That's terrible," Mom said.

It was true, though. Isa's parents had good jobs. They lived in a nice house. Aunt Tati and her husband had so-so jobs. They lived in a small house. They had bad luck.

"Rafe gives me the creeps," Eddie said. "I got out of there fast."

8

A DARK IDEA

Isa went to her room. She had homework. But she couldn't think about anything. Her cousin. Hm. A dark idea came to her. Her heart began to race.

Mom kept a photo album. Isa went to the bookshelf. There! The album. She found a school picture of Rafe. It was old. Two years, maybe. He hadn't changed much.

same long hair

same attitude

Isa could not sleep that night. She tossed and turned. All she could think about was Rafe. How bitter he was. How angry he was. How he seemed happy that Grandma's picture was missing. It was weird.

Isa looked for Sandy at school. When she saw Sandy, she rushed over. She pulled out the photo of her cousin. Showed it to Sandy. "Does this boy look like the gardener? The one in our backyard?" she asked. "Could this be him?"

Sandy stared at the photo. "This guy is younger. I don't know. Maybe."

"This picture is old," Isa said.

"Well, it does look like him. Kinda. I'm not sure. He was clipping the bushes way back. He was in a shadow," Sandy said. "I'm not sure. But it could be him. Who is he?"

Isa did not want to tell anybody about her fears. It wasn't fair to point fingers. Especially on a hunch. "Just some guy I used to know. Thanks, Sandy."

"Have you told your grandma? About the picture being gone?" Sandy asked.

Isa shook her head. "Grandma is coming over on Sunday. We'll have to tell her then. She goes right to the living room. Always. First she looks at her picture. Then she says a prayer for Grandpa."

Saturday was a cool, sunny day. Isa figured Rafe would be skateboarding with his friends. She knew the usual place. Isa got a frozen yogurt at the corner. Then she waited for the skateboarders to arrive.

Brain freeze!

Perfect!

yummy toppings

FROZEN YOGURT

The boys came carrying their boards. One of them was Rafe.

"Hi, Rafe," Isa called to him. She walked toward him.

He stopped. Looked at Isa. It was a hard look. They had not seen each other in a while. "What's up?" he said finally.

Uhhh... hi, Isa.

"I need to talk to you," Isa said.

"I got no time for talk," Rafe snapped.

"I'm skateboarding with my buds."

"You better make time. It's about Grandma's stolen picture," Isa said. She tried to look tough.

Rafe shrugged. They walked to the curb. Sat down.

"Make it quick," Rafe said. He seemed nervous. He was picking at his fingers. He looked tough. The kind of boy Isa avoided.

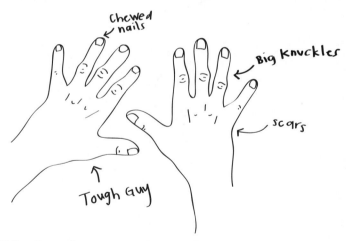

Chewed nails

Big Knuckles

scars

Tough Guy

"My brother saw you the other day. He said you seemed happy. Happy about the

52

picture being stolen," Isa said.

Rafe swallowed. "So what?" he said. He picked at one finger until it bled. Something was going on. That was for sure.

"Rafe," Isa said. "Somebody saw you at our house. That night." Her heart was pounding. She was scared. But she didn't want to show it. She looked at him. Waiting.

"That's crazy," Rafe cried. "Nobody saw me. I didn't do nothing!"

"You were pretending to clip our hedge. Then you snuck inside. Stole the picture," Isa said.

Main Library

Checked out to GAYE2102
05/23/2017 10.52 AM

Checked Out Today

Stolen treasure
Barcode: 33111007918010
Date due: 06/13/2017 11:59 PM

Fargo Public Library - Main Library
102 3 ST N
FARGO, ND 58102
701-241-1472
http://www.fargolibrary.org/

9
WE'RE NOT NOBODIES

Rafe turned pale. His lip shook. "That's a lie. A dirty lie!"

"Did your mom tell you to do it? Did she want to make trouble for us? 'Cause she's jealous of Mom," Isa said. "It's a crime, Rafe. You know it's a serious crime. Breaking into a house. Stealing."

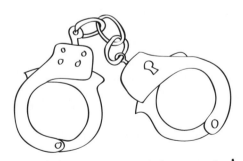

Break the law... get arrested.

Rafe looked scared. "You tell your parents?"

"Not yet. I haven't told anybody," Isa said.

"My mom doesn't know anything about it," Rafe said. "It's just something I did. Grandma doesn't respect my mom. Never has. Grandma loves your mom. She's her pet. Mom is always crying about it. My mom's been hurt a lot. I'm tired of it," he blurted out.

Grandma's Pet

"Rafe, you have to give it back," Isa said.

"My mom wanted to have the picture in our house. She thought we could have it for half the year. Then you guys have it the other half. Why not share? Mom even made a place for it in our living room. How come everything goes your way? Don't you think we got feelings too? You got it all. Even the picture. It's like my mom is nobody."

Rafe was shaking. He was breathing hard. "Mom tells me all the time. How it was when she was a kid. How your mom was the princess. My mom was nobody. So I wanted to do something. Something so Grandma knows you aren't so hot. You let the picture get stolen. You're not perfect. I wanted Grandma to hurt. Aunt Maria to hurt. Just like my mom has been hurting."

Isa hated what Rafe did. But she felt sorry for him too. Grandma probably never knew how Aunt Tati felt. Grandma meant no harm. She just didn't know. Just like Isa didn't know. Isa didn't know Gina was sad. Isa always won. Gina was always second.

"You gonna tell?" Rafe asked. "You gonna call the cops?"

"Give the picture back today. I won't tell anybody. Grandma is coming for dinner tomorrow. I want her picture to be where it was," Isa said.

"Okay. Tonight. I'll stick it in the shed after it gets dark," Rafe said.

"It's not damaged or anything. Is it?" Isa asked.

"Nah. I was real careful. I was gonna pretend I found it in a trash bin. That I saved it. I thought that would show Grandma. That we're not nobodies," Rafe said.

Rafe got up slowly. He looked right at Isa. "You're pretty. Your mom is pretty.

Grandma is pretty. She is beautiful in the picture. Mom's not pretty like that. But that doesn't mean I don't love her. That doesn't mean she's not worth anything," Rafe said.

"I understand," Isa said.

"Okay. Tonight. Right when it gets dark," Rafe said.

"Thanks. I'm sorry. You know. For everything," Isa said.

10
I HEARD SOMETHING

Isa was very nervous about that night. She worried that Rafe would not keep his word. What if he did not show up? What if he was lying about the picture? What if he had thrown it away? Maybe the treasure was gone forever.

Isa went outside late in the day. It was still light. But the moon was already up. Soon, it would be dark. Isa could hardly wait.

Mom looked out the patio door. "You seem so jumpy. Are you okay? You've been pacing."

"I'm just worried. About tomorrow," Isa said.

Mom nodded. "I am too. I still don't know what to say. I'm so angry with myself. Why didn't I fasten the frame to the wall? Did I leave the sliding doors unlocked? Why?"

"Come on, Maria," Dad said gently. "Don't beat yourself up. Who would ever dream that someone would steal that picture? It means the world to us. But it isn't worth any money. Why would a thief bother with it?"

At dinner, Isa could hardly eat. Eddie was chowing down. But the sight of food made Isa sick. She wished she could be like

Eddie. The troubles of the world washed over him. Just like waves on a sandy beach.

The sun went down. Dinner was over. Isa heard something outside. She clasped her hands. She froze. "Uh, I'm going outside," she said. "I heard … I think an animal might be out there."

Isa grabbed a flashlight. She ran outside. She rushed to the shed. Her heart was pounding. She saw something wrapped in a blanket. She opened one corner. "The picture! The picture's back!" she yelled.

Everyone ran outside.

"Thank God," Mom cried. Tears were running down her face.

Dad took the picture inside. Inspected it. Hung it back up.

"The thief must have felt guilty. He brought it back." Mom smiled.

The next day, Grandma came for dinner. Everyone was happier than usual. Something precious was lost. Then found. After eating, Isa and Grandma took a walk. It was such a lovely evening.

Isa began to tell Grandma about Gina. How jealous she always was. How Isa did not enter the poster contest. She wanted Gina to win. Isa told Grandma how happy

64

Gina was. How they were friends again.

Then Isa said, "You know, Grandma. We've had your picture in our house. It's been a long time. Ten years. I know Aunt Tati would love to have it. She even made a place for it in her living room."

Grandma turned. "I never knew she felt that way. It would be great to share. What does your mom think?"

"She thinks it's great. She wants to share."

"Then it's done," Grandma said.

Isa gave her grandma a big hug.

The next week Aunt Tati hung the picture in her living room. Everyone thought it looked great. Just as nice as before. Tati and Mom gave each other big hugs. Grandma wiped away a tear. Her girls would be friends again. She was sure of it.